PUSS IN BOOTS

Retold by Susan Saunders
Illustrated by Elizabeth Miles

SCHOLASTIC INC.

New York Toronto London Auckland Sydney

To James McBride
—S.S.

For my sister, Katy
—E.M.

ISBN 0-590-41888-2

Text copyright © 1989 by Susan Saunders.

Illustrations copyright © 1989 by Elizabeth J. Miles.

All rights reserved. Published by Scholastic Inc.

12 11 10 9 8 7 6 5 4 3 2 1   9/8 0 1 2 3 4/9

Printed in the U.S.A.   23

First Scholastic printing, August 1989

Once there was a very old miller
with three young sons.
"When I die," the miller told them,
"as everyone must,
I will have only three things to leave you:
my mill, my donkey, and Puss, my faithful cat."
To his oldest son, the miller said,
he would leave the mill.
To his middle son, he would leave
his strong but gentle donkey.
All that was left for the youngest son
was Puss the cat.

"Together, my brothers can make
   a nice living for themselves,"
   the youngest son thought.
"They will use the donkey to grind
   the farmers' grain at the mill.
   The farmers will pay them well.
   But what will I have?
   After I have eaten the cat
   and made mittens out of his fur,
   I will starve to death!"

   Not long after that, the miller died.
   His two older sons hitched
   the donkey to the millstone
   and ground the farmers' grain.
   Before the youngest son could make the family cat
   into cutlets, however, Puss spoke up.

"Just give me a sturdy sack, Master,
  and a pair of boots for walking in the woods.
  I will show you that your share
  is the best share of all."

What did the youngest son have to lose?
He could always eat the cat later.
He found a sturdy sack
with strings to pull it closed,
and a small pair of high boots.

Puss tugged the boots on with a toothy grin.
He hung the sack around his neck
and set out for the woods.

On the way, Puss filled the
sack with tender green grass.
Then he found a shady bank
dotted with rabbit holes.
There he placed the open sack
on the ground.
He stretched out next to it,
lying as quietly as he was able.
Puss did not so much as twitch a whisker.
He did not even breathe.

Before long, a foolish young rabbit
crawled out of its hole.
"A dead cat is a good cat," the rabbit murmured.
It hopped right into the sack filled with grass.
Mister Puss pulled the strings tight.
Presto! The tasty rabbit was trapped!

Well pleased with himself,
Puss hung the sack around his neck.
He hurried straight to the palace
of the king and demanded to see him.
"Tell the king I have a gift from my master,"
said Puss.

When the king heard of a talking cat
wearing high boots and asking to see him,
he ordered, "Bring him to me!"

Puss marched into the throne room
and made a low bow.
"I have for you, Sire," Puss said,
"a present from the Duke of Carabas."
(The Duke of Carabas?
That was the fancy name
Puss made up for his master.)
"Tell your master," said the king,
"that I thank him for his rabbit
and his thoughtfulness.
I will remember his name."
"Thank you, Sire," said the cat.

Only a week had passed
when Puss hid himself in a field of wheat.
He filled his sack with the grain
and left it standing open.

Before long, two greedy partridges
strolled into the sack,
and Puss pulled it closed.

Once again, he was off to the palace
to see the king.
The king was very fond of partridges.
He gave the cat a small gift
to take back to the duke.

Now, the king had one daughter,
the most beautiful princess in the world.
And Puss heard that the king planned
to take a trip with her along the river.

"If you do as I tell you,"
  the cat said to his master,
"your fortune will be made.
  You must swim in the river
  at the spot I point out.
  Leave the rest to me."

The miller's son did as Puss told him.
While he was swimming,
the king's coach rolled past.

Puss shouted at the top of his voice,
"Help! Help! The Duke of Carabas is drowning!"

The king remembered the name,
  and he remembered Puss.
"Save the duke!" said the king to his guards.

While the guards pulled the duke
from the river,
Puss told the king a long story
about robbers who had stolen
the duke's clothes while he swam.
In truth, Puss had hidden
the clothes under a rock.
But the king took Puss at his word.
He sent for a fine suit
to be brought from the palace.

The duke was a handsome young man.
When the princess saw him dressed
in the fine suit of clothes,
she fell deeply in love.
The king invited him to ride in their coach.
He invited Puss as well,
but the cat had other business to tend to.

Puss ran ahead of the king and his guests
to a field where some farmers were plowing.

"My good fellows," said Puss.
"If you do not tell the king
  that this field belongs
  to the Duke of Carabas …
  you will be chopped into pieces, like mincemeat."

Soon the king came along in his coach.
"To whom does this field belong?" he called out.

"To the Duke of Carabas!"
  the farmers all answered together.

"You have some fine land,"
  said the king to the duke.

Farther up the river, Puss found
a group of country folk picking peaches.

"Listen to me," the cat said to the country folk.
"You must say that these orchards
   belong to the Duke of Carabas ...
   or you will be chopped into pieces,
   like mincemeat."

When the king stopped his coach
to ask who owned the orchards,
the country folk shouted,
"The Duke of Carabas, Sire!"

The cat stayed one jump ahead of the coach
on its journey.
And the king was amazed by the wealth
of the Duke of Carabas.

Finally Puss arrived at a marvelous castle.
The castle belonged to
a dreadful but very rich ogre.
He owned all the lands Puss had claimed
for the Duke of Carabas.

Puss had heard of the ogre, and of his terrible magic.
But Puss walked across the drawbridge
as bravely as he could.

The ogre was waiting on the other side.

"I know about your wonderful powers,"
said Puss. "Is it true that you can change yourself
into any animal you please?"

"It is true!" the ogre roared.
And in the blink of an eye,
he turned himself into a huge lion.

Puss was so frightened
that he leaped onto the roof,
his boots sliding on the tiles.
The ogre bellowed with laughter,
and changed himself back.

Puss took a deep breath.
"I have been told," he said,
"that you can also take the shape
  of a very small animal—
  a rat, perhaps, or even a mouse.
But I can not believe it."

"Believe it!" thundered the ogre.
  In a flash, he turned into a tiny mouse,
  skittering around on the cobblestones.
  Just as quickly, Puss jumped down from the roof.
  He pounced on the mouse and gobbled it up!

  Puss had hardly finished washing his whiskers
  when the king's coach rumbled through the gates.
  Puss ran to meet it.

"Welcome, Your Majesty," he cried,
"to the castle of the Duke of Carabas!"

"What?" said the king.
"This splendid castle is yours, Duke?
  I would like nothing better than
  to go inside and look around."

The duke led them
to a great hall
at the top of the castle
where a table had been set
with a glorious feast.

After the king had dined
on peaches and peacocks,
he turned to his host:
"Duke, it would make me most happy
  to have you for a son-in-law."

That very evening the Duke of Carabas
married the beautiful princess.

Puss became a cat
of great importance,
who hunted mice rarely,
and then only for fun.